30007000261239

E
W
Weldon, Fay.

Nobody likes me!

2888 $16.96

DATE DUE	BORROWER'S NAME	ROOM NO
	Heather	KO
	TJ	KG
MAY 40	Titeana	4-H
	Libby.	
OCT 3 06	Kal	K

2888

30007000261239
E
W
Weldon, Fay.

Nobody likes me!

**LAWRENCE SCHOOL LIBRARY
MIDDLETOWN, CT 06457**

902680 01696 42624A 43112E   007

Fay Weldon
NOBODY LIKES ME!
Illustrated by Claudio Muñoz

The Bodley Head

London

1 3 5 7 9 10 8 6 4 2

Copyright © text Fay Weldon 1997

Copyright © illustrations Claudio Muñoz 1997

Fay Weldon and Claudio Muñoz have asserted their rights
under the Copyright, Designs and Patents Act, 1988 to be identified
as the author and illustrator of this work

Text originally published as Party Puddle © 1989 by HarperCollins.

This edition with revised text and new illustrations first published in
the United Kingdom 1997 by The Bodley Head Children's Books, Random House,
20 Vauxhall Bridge Road, London SW1V 2SA

Random House Australia (Pty) Limited
20 Alfred Street, Milsons Point, Sydney, New South Wales 2061, Australia

Random House New Zealand Limited
18 Poland Road, Glenfield, Auckland 10, New Zealand

Random House South Africa (Pty) Limited, PO Box 337,
Bergvlei 2012, South Africa

Random House UK Limited Reg. No. 954009

A CIP record for this book is available from the British Library

ISBN 0 370 324625

Printed in Dubai by
Oriental Press (Dubai)

On Tuesday Rex received an invitation to a party. The card was really interesting. It was yellow and mauve in the middle and had green deckled edges. But Rex tore it up and stamped on the pieces. That was on the way home from school, when he was in a bad temper.

'What shall we do with you?' asked his mother. She had been to the dentist and was wearing her best red dress and her teeth were very white.

'Do what you like!' said Rex. 'I'm a big brown bear and I'll eat you up and every scrap of your best red dress!'

He stamped with his black shoe on the grey mud at the
bottom of a silvery puddle and splashed his little sister's
new pink coat by mistake; but it wasn't by mistake. His
little sister went on smiling with her little pink mouth,
so he splashed some more until she cried, with a thin,
pale-blue sound.

'You shan't go to the party,' said his mother. 'Who'd
want you at a party? You've torn up the invitation anyway.'

Rex ran up the path and into his house and crept into
the dark beneath his bed like a bear into his den. He
pulled the brown furry quilt off the top of the bed and
all his toys and books fell down in front of him and
Rex didn't pick them up. No. He rolled himself in the
quilt, right up against the walls beneath the bed where
it was blackest, and there he stayed till suppertime.

Sometimes he roared a black sound like a bear who is angry and sometimes he yelped a white sound like a bear who is wounded and sometimes he was silent.

His mother opened the door and put some bread and
water on the carpet, but went away quickly before Rex
could eat her up. He was very dangerous.

Rex fell into a sleep that was brown and red and purple at
the edges, until a white bright dream came towards him.

In the dream, Rex was going to a party up a long flight of steps to a grand grey house. A footman opened the door and all the children inside were dressed in white, in the party clothes of long ago, and so was Rex. Each child had a nanny and so did he. She had a kind face and very white teeth. Everyone made room for Rex at the long table, though he wasn't expected.

They ate jelly out of silver bowls and sugar plums from golden forks.
A lady in a pale sequined dress sat down at a white piano and sang a
high, white song which Rex loved.

But then the notes became hard and wrong and she pointed straight at Rex and called out:

'Look at that boy! He's wearing black. We don't want him at our party!'

Rex looked down and saw he was wearing his black school trousers again, and they were so short he could see his ankles, so he ran out of the house as fast as he could. He looked behind and saw that all the nannies and all the children were running after him, but white and bright and distant like a comet stream.

Rex ran till he came to a white
cliff halfway round the world,
at the edge of a Northern sea,
and there on a rock a
lighthouse stood.

Inside, the sea-captain's wife was giving a party for her three little girls;
Faith, Hope and Charity. They had yellow pigtails and big round eyes,
like china dolls.

'Where is your invitation?' asked the sea-captain's wife.

'I tore it up,' said Rex.

'Never mind,' said the sea-captain's wife. 'You're welcome anyway.'

All the girls at the party wore pink and white check and so did Rex. They ate golden-brown fishfingers and browny-gold chipped potatoes, still glistening from the chip pan. The tablecloth was pink and white and so were the cushions and the carpet and sometimes it was hard to see where one stopped and the other began. After tea they played Pass-the-Parcel. Rex was lucky and the music kept stopping just for him. He was about to unwrap the last piece of pink and white paper, when he noticed he was wearing his grey school jersey again. It was too small. There was a gap of shirt before his trousers.

'That boy is an imposter!' shrieked the sea-captain's wife. 'He didn't even show his invitation.'

Rex tried to explain that he had torn
it up but the words wouldn't come.
So he quickly ran out of the lighthouse
and along the edge of the cliff and the
three girls ran after him and as they ran
they smiled with their little pink mouths.
The parcel slipped out of Rex's arms and
the wind caught the last piece of pink and
white paper and whipped it up into the grey
and white seascape sky. The present in the parcel
was a giant egg, greeny-white. The egg cracked and
out pushed a golden eagle with bright, friendly yellow
eyes, which fluffed itself out to an enormous, feathery size.
   'We wild things must keep together,' shrieked the eagle
and snatched Rex up in padded claws, in the nick of time.

The eagle carried Rex over purple snow-capped mountains and green velvet plains, and set him down in a tall, thin, glittering city where slender buildings pierced a misty sky. 'Last chance!' squawked the eagle and flew off.

A high-speed lift zoomed Rex to the penthouse of the tallest, thinnest building of all. The building was made of glass and the lift was made of mirrors and wherever you looked you saw a hundred of yourself.

The lift stopped, the doors opened, and there was a room where a millionaire was giving a party for his little boy. The children wore sweatshirts, jeans and trainers and so did Rex. Everyone was eating hamburgers and chips.

What a party that was! No-one sat down. Grown-ups and children danced on a floor which splodged into rainbow colours at every footfall. The music grew louder, coloured lights flashed quicker and brighter and Rex was just about to take another hamburger, when the music stopped and everyone was still and silent, staring at Rex.

'Careful,' said the millionaire. 'Careful! That isn't a boy, it's a bear!
And it's dangerous!'

Rex looked down and saw the millionaire was right. He roared so
loudly everyone was frightened and shrunk into corners like stick
insects. It was easy.

But Rex was ashamed of himself and his mother wouldn't like it if he ate them all up, so he ran to the window and clambered out and shinned down the building easily with his long strong arms. But even so he was all alone and the starry sky was far above and the pale ground far below and his arms grew weak and he thought he might fall.

His sleep was brown and red and purple at the edges opening into patches of dark under-bed and carpet green, and his mother was pulling him out from underneath. She was wearing her black best evening dress and ruby red earrings and her clickety-clack silver sandals.

'You mustn't worry about the invitation,'
she said. 'We can ask for another one.'

She took off Rex's school shoes and said, 'How scuffed they are, and beginning to be tight.'

She took off Rex's black school trousers and said, 'These have got to be much too short. I can see your ankles.'

She took off the rest of everything and said, 'How you've grown lately, Rex, and I hadn't even noticed. I've been so busy with other things. We'll go shopping tomorrow after school. I'll leave your little sister at home. We'll have tea in a shop, with hamburgers.'

She put on his pyjamas and laid him on the bed and put the brown furry quilt over him – the one he'd had since he was a baby – and said,

'This raggedy old fur quilt! High time it went too!'
But Rex clung to it tightly, so she said, 'Well, I daresay not.'

Rex woke on Wednesday happy and good and went to the party on Saturday dressed up in a brown bear suit his mother had made, but nothing unusual happened at all.